THE DOG
from Arf! Arf!
to Zzzzzz

THE DOG
Artlist Collection

THE DOG

from

Arf!

Arf!

to

Zzzzzz

HarperCollins*Publishers*

*Dedicated to
the dog lovers
of the world*

A

Arf! *Arf!*

B

Beg.

C

Come!

D

Down.

E

Eat

F

Fetch!

G

Good
dog.

Itch,
itch,
itch

J

Jump!

K

Kiss,
kiss

L

Lie down.

N

No!

Oops

P

Paw

Q

Quiet.

R

Roll over and over. and over.

S

Sit! Stay!

T

Tail

U

Upside пʍоp

V

Vroom! Vroom!

W

Wag, wag, wag

X

**X marks
the spot.**

Y

Yawn

Z

Zzzzz

Breeds